Ellie May

on Presidents' Day

Ellie May
on presidents' Day

Hillary Homzie

illustrated by Jeffrey Ebbeler

ini Charlesbridge

Published by Charlesbridge
85 Main Street
Watertown, MA 02472
(617) 926-0329
www.charlesbridge.com

Library of Congress Cataloging-in-Publication Data
Names: Homzie, Hillary, author. | Ebbeler, Jeffrey, illustrator.
Title: Ellie May on Presidents' Day / Hillary Homzie; illustrated by Jeffrey Ebbeler.
Description: Watertown, MA: Charlesbridge, [2018] | Summary: Ellie May really wants
    to be her second-grade class's flag leader during the Pledge of Allegiance, however
    her enthusiasm and hyperactivity keep getting in the way, both in school and at
    home—but maybe learning everything about various presidents, dressing the part,
    or pleading her case will finally get her teacher to pick her, rather than the well-
    behaved Ava.
Identifiers: LCCN 2017055118 (print) | LCCN 2017057121 (ebook) |
    ISBN 9781632896759 (ebook) | ISBN 9781632896766 (ebook pdf) |
    ISBN 9781580898195 (reinforced for library use) | ISBN 9781580899284 (softcover)
Subjects: LCSH: Presidents' Day—Juvenile fiction. | Enthusiasm—Juvenile fiction.
    | Self-control—Juvenile fiction. | Families—Juvenile fiction. | Elementary schools—
    Juvenile fiction. | CYAC: Presidents' Day—Fiction. | Enthusiasm—Fiction.
    | Self-control—Fiction. | Family life—Fiction. | Schools—Fiction.
Classification: LCC PZ7.H7458 (ebook) | LCC PZ7.H7458 El 2018 (print) | DDC
    813.54 [Fic]—dc23
LC record available at https://lccn.loc.gov/2017055118

Printed in China
(hc) 10 9 8 7 6 5 4 3 2 1
(sc) 10 9 8 7 6 5 4 3 2 1

Illustrations done in black acrylic paint on hot press Fabriano paper and shaded digitally
Display type set in Canvas by Yellow Design Studio
Text type set in Calisto MT by Monotype Corporation
Printed by 1010 Printing International Limited in Huizhou, Guangdong, China
Production supervision by Brian G. Walker
Designed by Diane M. Earley

To my nieces Sarah, Jane and Clara, future triplet leaders of the world—H. H.

For Olivia—J. E.

chapter one
My Pledge

"Who wants to be flag leader?" asked Ms. Silva first thing Monday morning.

I sprang out of my seat and shouted, "Me! Me! Me!" My arms swished like windshield wipers. The whole class laughed.

Ms. Silva pointed to my desk. "Ellie May, body in chair, please." Then my teacher smiled at a girl across the room. A girl who was not swishing. A girl who was quietly sitting. "Ava will

1

be our flag leader," said Ms. Silva. "Let's give her a big ten-finger woo."

All the kids held up their hands. They wiggled their fingers and shouted, "Woo, woo, woo!" Even Lizzy—my best friend in the whole entire class—played along. But not me. I kept my body in chair and my hands super still.

Ava strolled to the front of the class and stood next to the flag. Everyone was silent. She lifted her hand to start the Pledge of Allegiance, and the rest of the class joined in. Ava had already been flag leader twice since winter break. And so had Lizzy. I hadn't been flag leader once in February or for months. I felt all fizzled and flat.

After the pledge Ms. Silva tapped the calendar. "Next Monday we won't be here. The school will be closed in honor of Presidents' Day, a very special holiday. Throughout the week, we will celebrate our presidents."

My belly got fluttery. There were only four more days this week to be flag leader before a very special holiday. I'd be a good flag leader. For one, I have a loud voice. Plus, I know how to stand up straight.

Over some holidays kids get to go to National Parks like Yosemite to see waterfalls or Muir Woods to see really tall trees. They brag about it during show-and-tell. But my family doesn't go away much in the winter. And as far as I knew, we weren't going anywhere over Presidents' Day weekend. I'd at least like to get to be flag leader for the holiday.

"Today we will learn more about Presidents' Day and what it means to have character," said Ms. Silva. "People with character do the right thing. They are good examples. Like our flag leaders. And"—she pointed to posters of presidents on the bulletin board—"like many of our country's great leaders."

Above me, the red, white, and blue flag flew.
I placed my right hand over my heart. That's when
a plan started to form. I made my own pledge.

This week I will be flag leader.

Chapter Two
Monkey-bar Business

During recess a gazillion kids played on the blacktop. Others zoomed on the field. And tons swung on the monkey bars. The sun was out and the sky was a happy blue.

The flag flapped on the flagpole. Of course this made me think of being flag leader the week before the Presidents' Day holiday.

Holiday. What a great word. A really happy word.

My throat went squeeze-y, which happens when I'm excited and worried. I needed to talk to my best friend.

Lizzy sat by herself on a picnic table, looking at a book. Only it wasn't an actual book. She was chewing on a pencil and studying a picture in her sketchbook. It was a drawing of fairies fighting monsters who have bad manners.

I whooshed up behind her and tapped her on the head.

Lizzy jerked back. Her pencil flew off the table. Her sketchbook went *ka-thunk* onto the ground.

"You scared me!" said Lizzy. "Why'd you do that?"

Ducking under the picnic table, I grabbed Lizzy's stuff. "Here!" I said, handing the sketchbook and pencil back to her. I had to raise my voice over the horses running by. Not real

6

ones. Jamila and her friends were clip-clopping like pretend horses.

"I tapped you so you wouldn't be scared," I explained. "That's the whole point. So you know somebody's behind you."

Sometimes Lizzy needed things explained to her. "If I wanted to really scare you," I said, "I would have dropped a rubber spider on you and shouted, 'Boo!' But I didn't do any of those things."

"Gosh, thanks," said Lizzy. She pushed up her glasses. They were aquamarine—the color a mermaid would wear. I really liked that.

"Hey, let's go there!" I pointed over to the monkey bars. I think better when I swing, and I needed to get my thoughts together for Lizzy.

"Well, I guess so."

We dodged a group of moaning third graders pretending to be zombies and swooshed over to the monkey bars. Actually I ran and Lizzy plodded.

"Hey, Frizzy Lizzy. Catch!" Mo called out from the basketball court. Whipping around, I watched Lizzy freeze. Playing catch in any way, shape, or form was her least favorite thing. Her bottom lip quivered.

"Put out your hands!" I hollered.

She didn't budge.

Mo threw the basketball right toward Lizzy.

"Move!" I yelled.

The ball was going to blast her in the head!

I zoomed in front of Lizzy, jumped up, and caught the ball. Then I hurled it back. "Leave us alone, Mo!

"He's just jealous," I told Lizzy. "Because your name has z's in it. Which jazzes everything up. Mo's name just has boring letters."

"Thanks, Ellie May," whispered Lizzy. "Z is my favorite letter."

Grabbing Lizzy's hand, I pulled her to the

monkey bars and explained my plan. "I want to be flag leader on Presidents' Day," I admitted. "Well, one of the days this week. Since we don't go to school on Presidents' Day."

Lizzy grabbed the bar facing me. She didn't swing. She just hung there. "Okaaaay," she said.

"So can you tell me how you got to be flag leader so many times?" I swung to the end of the monkey bars in two seconds flat.

"I raised my hand." Lizzy let go of the bar and dropped down. "That's how."

Pablo jumped up to grab the bars. He blocked me from going across.

"Move!" I said.

He dropped back down. "Go fast then."

I monkey-ed across the bars real quick. "*I* raise *my* hand," I said to Lizzy, "but Ms. Silva never calls on me. She hasn't in months."

"That's 'cause you're a weirdo," said Pablo.

"Takes one to know one." I stuck out my tongue at him. Pablo stuck out his tongue at me and made a silly face. We both laughed. Then he swung across the monkey bars and raced off to the basketball court.

"Maybe you're just a little *too* enthusiastic," Lizzy said. "You have

to have real good behavior, Ellie May. Sometimes you're loud. You talk when the teacher is talking. You always talk in line. Remember when you pretended to be a scorpion and stung everyone? Or the time you played with the automatic soap dispenser and foamed up the counter? Or when you drank tomato soup out of a straw?" Wow. Lizzy sure did remember everything.

"Yeah, I remember," I grumbled, hooking my legs on the bar. I swung upside down so fast that I almost went right side up.

Lizzy frowned. "Basically, Ellie May, you need to sit and do what Ms. Silva tells you."

"You sound just like Ava!"

"Yeah, well, guess who always gets to be flag leader?"

"Okay. Okay. Okay. I get it, thanks." Then I studied Ava. She was nearby, playing foursquare and yelling at Owen for cheating.

"Look at me right now and look at Ava," I said. "I'm swinging and using a very nice indoor voice, even though I'm outside. Am I yelling like Ava? No. But Ms. Silva can't hear me using a good voice because she eats lunch during recess." I looked around. "Only the yard-duty ladies can see all my goodness."

"It's not all about just how you sound or move," said Lizzy. "You have to be a good person. Like do good stuff, Ellie May."

"Right. Good stuff. Good *president* stuff," I said, pulling myself up through the monkey bars. "I can do that."

Chapter Three
Poster Projects

On Tuesday morning I wasn't picked for flag leader. Pablo was picked instead. For a moment I felt like an old piece of lettuce—wilted and sad. Then I knew exactly what I needed to do. If I acted like one of our former, famous presidents, I'd become flag leader. After writer's workshop we made posters of symbols for Presidents' Day Week. Pablo picked the Liberty Bell. That's a symbol of independence, even though it doesn't ring any more because it has a zig-zaggy crack.

You can see the bell in Pennsylvania. Ms. Silva said that James Buchanan is the only president we've ever elected from that state.

I didn't know what symbol to draw. It needed to be ten-finger-woo good. It needed to be good enough for a president. I decided to walk around to see everyone's posters.

Ava drew a beady-eyed bald eagle. "It looks so real," I told her. "He's a bald eagle so you better make him a wig too." Ava shook her head.

Nearby Jamila drew a horse with a flow-y mane. "It's the state animal of New Jersey," she explained. She told me Grover Cleveland was the only president born in New Jersey.

14

We don't even live in New Jersey, but Jamila is horse crazy. She puts horses on everything, even her hands. There aren't even any horses in Pineview, which is a silly name for our town because there aren't too many views of pine trees either. We live in southern California, so there are mostly palm trees and stuff. I don't think we'll get horses anytime soon, because my dad says we don't live near farms.

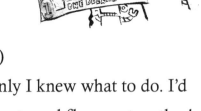

Lizzy drew Independence Hall, and Owen sketched the Statue of Liberty.

Mo made money. And so did Max, of course. (Max copies everything Mo does.)

Cha-ching! Suddenly I knew what to do. I'd draw the flag! Presidents and flags go together!

Whenever you see a president, I bet a flag is nearby. Woodrow Wilson was the president during the first Flag Day—the holiday that celebrates when our country officially adopted its flag.

I got to work right away and made my flag all razzle-dazzle. But I didn't add too many stripes. Since I heard my mom once say that too many stripes is called busy. Plus I made more stars for extra sparkle and shine! Presidents are stars.

Ava frowned at my poster. "That's wrong, Ellie May. For your information, you need thirteen stripes. And fifty stars on the flag. One for every state." Shoot, I didn't even think to count out what's on the actual flag.

"Ha ha ha, I was just making a joke," I said. "I'm making my real poster next."

"You're lying, Ellie May," said Ava. "That was your real poster."

"I'm not a liar. Just you wait and see!"

A little part of me knew I should have taken more time on the poster. But still it wasn't that messed up.

I wondered why Ava had to call me out on everything. My mom says sometimes people bug you when they're just jealous. But I don't think Ava is jealous of me.

Maybe I'm just a little bit jealous of her, though. Ms. Silva does pick her for everything, especially for flag leader.

chapter four
chop 'Til you Drop

Now it was already Wednesday, and I had to do my poster . . . again! I made it look extra good, with thirteen stripes, even though that's an unlucky number. Unlucky for me especially, because I didn't get picked for flag leader. Jamila did.

I didn't like that my chances to get picked were running out. And I really didn't like Ava saying I lied. George Washington didn't lie. He was a president, the very first one, and his face is on a big rock! I saw it on a family vacation.

George Washington was said to be honest.
On TV I saw a cartoon about George Washington
admitting to his dad that he chopped down a
cherry tree with his brand-new axe. His father
was really happy he didn't lie.

I wanted to be like George Washington. During
reading time I decided to make myself more like
our first president, so I could prove I was honest.
And so Ava wouldn't call me a liar again.

A little tree stood in a pot inside our classroom
on a windowsill. It looked like a cactus actually.
But I could pretend it was a cherry tree.

"Woo-wee. Look at me!" I shouted, waving.
"I'm going to chop down this cherry tree like
George Washington!"

"That's a myth. That means it's not true,"
called out Ava.

"Well, I learned it was true on TV," I said.

Ava put her hands on her hips. "Over time

myths can get spread. That doesn't mean they are real."

"Well, watch this!"

Lots of kids watched me. Lizzy got wide-eyed and looked worried.

I didn't have an axe. So I karate chopped the tree with my hand. *Kaboom!* The dry, brittle plant split in two.

"Ow ow ow ow owwwwwww!" I screamed.

Ms. Silva shot up from behind her desk.

She hurried over to me. "Are you okay, Ellie May?"

"Yeah."

"Was that a smart choice?" she asked as she propped up the cactus.

I shook my head.

Ms. Silva picked up a dustbin and a broom and handed them to me. "Why don't you clean this up."

I could feel my face getting all warm. I felt so dumb. I swept really hard, only I got dirt all over my shirt. That plant was getting back at me. But that wasn't all. Ms. Silva strode over to the class behavior chart. She grabbed the clothespin with my name on it and moved it from the green good square to the orange not-so-good square. Orange means a warning.

The next square is red and is called the "teacher's choice." That meant the teacher would choose what kind of punishment you get.

"Ellie May thinks she's presidential because she acted out a myth about George Washington," Ava said. "Something that never happened."

A whole bunch of kids giggled, especially Ava and Max. I plopped down in my seat.

Lizzy gave Ava and Max a mean look. "How do you know what happened back then?" she asked. "Were you alive back in the olden days?"

"Everyone quiet down," said Ms. Silva. "George Washington didn't chop down a tree. Everything we think we know about our presidents may not always be true," she added. "That's why we look to all kinds of books and sources to learn different perspectives. Often history is full of hidden stories and difficult realities." She pointed to the special library she'd put together of different books about our presidents. "A writer made up the cherry-tree story to try to emphasize what he thought was George Washington's honesty. If all of you want to be good leaders or honest, treat each other with equal respect, and just tell the truth."

"I can do that," I said. And I could.

I just had to figure out how.

chapter Five
something Red

On the bus home I thought about all the stuff we were learning in school. About symbols, myths, and presidents. And how much I wanted to be flag leader.

I did my second-best thinking on the bus. So that's when I got a great idea. What if I dressed up in red, white, and blue tomorrow? Just like a flag! Then maybe Ms. Silva would pick me to be flag leader.

At home I quickly said hi to my dad and Midge before racing upstairs. I needed something red. Like a sweater. Or leggings. I already had a white polo shirt and blue jeans. But nothing red. Well, okay, I had a red shirt, but it had holes.

On Lexie's bedroom door it said: *Keep out! Private Property!* Big sisters can be so dramatic. I ignored the sign and crept inside. Then I paused and listened for the thump of her feet on the stairs. She would be coming home soon from swim practice.

I heard the fridge open downstairs. And then the hum of the microwave. It sounded like Dad was making Midge a snack. *Whew, no Lexie!*

My sister's bedroom was even messier than mine. A bunch of clothes hung off a bedpost. Her comforter lay on the floor. On her dresser, the cup part of her swim trophy overflowed with pennies.

Yanking out the dresser's right bottom drawer, I pawed through Lexie's stuff. A peach lace-up shirt. A white top but with red cats all over it. A purple poncho.

On her bed she had a red sheet. But I couldn't wear a sheet.

I darted into her closet when Midge burst into the room.

"You can't be in here," she said, her cheeks full of pizza, her lips smeared with sauce.

She pointed to the sign on Lexie's door. Midge was three and couldn't read, but she knew what those letters meant. Diesel, our labradoodle, bounded right into the room and flopped onto the floor. "Nobody should be in here," Midge said. "Not even dogs."

"It's fine," I said.

"I'm going to tell Dad!" Midge grew a giant grin. She looked way too happy.

Ugh. Dad would give me a time-out. And take away my dessert.

"Don't you want to help your country?" I asked.

"Yes," said Midge. "Yes! Yes!" She licked her fingers. "What's a country?"

"It's a place where you live, Midge. Like a house only"—I spread out my arms—"way bigger."

"But I already have a house," said Midge. "Don't need a country. I'm going to tell!"

"*Shh!*" I said. "I'll give you one of my cookies at dinner tonight." Diesel's tail thumped.

"Okay!" shouted Midge.

I put my fingers to my lips. "You can be my helper. But you've got to keep it down. This is what we have to do. We have to look for something red. Because it's a color on the American flag. And I want to look just like the flag."

Midge pulled the red sheet off Lexie's bed. "Tada!"

I shook my head. "I can't wear a sheet to school, Miss Pizza Lips."

"That's mean talk. I'm going to tell on you." Midge made her screamy look. Her mouth opened wide. Diesel looked up at us in anticipation.

"Be quiet, Midge. Okay? C'mon. We'll play Pledge of Allegiance together. And you can be the flag. And I'll pledge to you. You have to be a real good pledger if you want to be flag leader."

I tied the sheet around her. "Now Midge," I instructed, "hold still. And stay quiet."

I made a loop. Then another. A knot. And then a double knot.

"It's too tight." Midge scowled.

"It's supposed to be," I explained, looking in the closet for something red to wear. "That way it won't fall off, okay?"

"Ever?"

I laughed. "Yes."

"Yay!" she shouted. "I get to wear a dress for forever!"

"No, Midge," I said in my calmest and most patient voice. "Not a dress. A flag. You are a flag." I opened the left bottom drawer of the dresser. Nothing red there either.

She gazed down at the sheet, dragging it around the floor. "Not a dress?"

"No, a flag. I've told you ten hundred times." I opened the upper right drawer of the dresser. Still nothing red.

"I'm a flag?" she asked.

"Yes!" I put my hand over my heart. Then I practiced saying the Pledge of Allegiance.

Midge wrinkled her forehead. "Why are you saying all those words?"

"Because you're very important. You're a flag! People look up to you. And say stuff. That's why flags are way up high."

"I'm high," said Midge, jumping.

"Not really," I said. "In school, flags are up

29

way higher, on flagpoles. So high, you would need a tall ladder."

"I go higher!" Midge bounced into the bottom drawer of the dresser.

The dresser wobbled.

She pulled herself up into the upper right drawer.

The dresser wobbled even more. Diesel stood up excitedly. He probably wanted to get on the dresser too.

"That's getting high, Midge," I said. The sheet dangled and swooshed.

She pushed herself up onto the top of the dresser and then stood up.

"Now I really high!" she shouted.

"Yes, Midge. You are. You're as tall as a pole." Her red sheet swished. I clapped.

"Ellie May, I'm big now," said Midge. "Bigger than you. Bigger than Lexie. Bigger than Mom. Bigger than Dad!" She jumped up and down.

"*Shhh!* Flags don't jump. Flags flap. They blow gently in the breeze." I puffed out my cheeks. "I'm the wind. And I'm going to blow so you can flap." I blew as hard as I could.

Midge jumped up and down on the dresser.

"Don't jump. Flap and sway." I flapped my arms and showed her.

Midge flapped her arms. *Flap. Flap. Flap.* She also jumped. This time the dresser really, *really* wobbled.

Lexie's swimming trophy toppled off with a bang! It hit the floor. The pennies toppled out. *Ping! Ping! Ping!* Diesel barked and barked.

"Uh-oh!" said Midge, looking down from the dresser.

"It's okay. It's okay," I said, scrambling to pick up the trophy and all the pennies.

That's when someone's footsteps thundered up the stairs.

Chapter Six
Honesty Is
the Best Policy

Dad rushed into the bedroom. "Midge, get down off that dresser."

"I can't," she said, flapping her arms. "I'm a flag. A flag's got to be high and flap!"

Dad carried Midge off the dresser.

Then Lexie burst into the room. She had a towel around her neck. Her hair was still wet from swim practice. "What happened?" Her eyes got real big. "My trophy!" she cried. She grabbed it out of my hands. "The dolphin's tail broke off!"

The dog nudged Dad's leg, trying to help. "Diesel, lie down," said Dad. Diesel lay down, his nose in his paws.

Dad put Midge down on the floor. He inspected the tail of the broken dolphin trophy. He scratched his beard. "I can glue it back, Lexie," he said gently.

Lexie slapped her hands on her hips. "Why are all my drawers open?"

"Maybe there was a teeny, tiny earthquake," I said.

"No! Ellie May opened them!" shouted Midge. She pointed her chubby finger at me. "She needed something red, and I needed to go up way high."

"You can't take my clothes without asking!" Lexie shouted. "And why is Midge wearing my sheet?"

I shrugged. "No idea."

"You told me to be a flag!" Midge cried out.

"Sounds like someone hasn't been telling the truth," Dad said in a calm voice. He looked right at me.

"Yeah, Ellie May," said Lexie. "You're such a liar." Then she turned to Midge. "You're messing up my sheet. Just wait until Mom gets home. She'll put you both on trial."

"No, she won't," I said. Mom's a lawyer, and Lexie likes to say stuff like she can bring us to court or put us in jail. But I know now that's not true. In real life she can only put us in time-out.

Dad peered at the clothes on the bedpost. "Lexie, you're also at fault here." He picked the comforter off the floor. "Maybe if you made your bed, your sheets wouldn't look like rags in the first place."

"It's not like I have time," Lexie huffed.

"You could get up earlier," said Dad. "You could make time." Kneeling down, he un-knotted

35

the sheet. "Midge, Ellie May, you can't go into Lexie's room. You can't step on her clothes. And you can't play dress-up with her sheets."

"It's not a dress, Daddy," said Midge. "It's a flag. Ellie May already told me ten hundred times."

"So what's all this about, Ellie May?" asked Dad. He tucked the sheet back onto Lexie's bed.

"This is about patriotism," I explained.

"It's about cookies!" said Midge.

"Explain," said Dad.

So I did. I told him everything. How I hadn't been flag leader. Not even once in February or for months. And how I wanted to be flag leader during the special week when we were celebrating Presidents' Day. "Plus, a flag leader gets to stand up in front of the class like in a play."

Dad said now he understood.

Then he calmed down Midge. He found a spare sheet she could wear.

He calmed down Lexie. "We can superglue the trophy," he explained. "And if we wash it in warm soapy water and polish it with a rag, it'll shine even more than it had before."

"Okay," said Lexie. She didn't look so slumpy any more.

"Ellie May, my office now, please."

I followed Dad.

"Do you think it was fair to go into Lexie's room without asking?" he asked, pushing aside a stack of papers on the chairs so we could sit. Dad's a writer, so it's his job to print out lots of paper.

I shook my head. "No."

"Should you be in someone's room without their permission?" he asked. I shook my head.

"Or take their belongings?"

"No," I said.

"And if someone asks you about it, should you lie or tell the truth?" he asked.

37

"Tell the truth," I said. I thought about it for a moment. "I should be honest. I know deep down how important honesty is. I'm going to tell the truth right now," I said, pausing.

"That's wonderful, Ellie May," said Dad. As he hugged me, his stubble tickled my cheek.

Afterward I went upstairs and knocked on Lexie's door.

"Come in," she called out. She sat on her bed. Diesel had his head on her lap, and she was petting him. "What is it, Ellie May?" Her voice sounded fizzled and flat.

"I'm sorry," I told her. "Super-duper sorry. I'll never go into your room and have Midge stand on top of your dresser and pretend to be a flag ever, ever, ever again. Please don't be mad."

"Fine." Lexie sighed.

"One more thing. Can you help me?" I asked. "I'm in a very big pickle." That's what my dad

says when he's got a problem. It doesn't mean you're really inside a pickle.

"Can you please, with a cherry—but not a cherry tree—on top, let me borrow something red? So I can look like the American flag tomorrow at school. Pretty please, with whipped cream and sprinkles on top?"

Lexie's lips pulled into an almost smile. "Ellie May, you can borrow these," she said, opening her drawer. She tossed a pair of red socks to me. "Just don't smell them up."

"I won't," I said. "Promise. I'll wash my feet before I even put them on so they'll smell like a summer day!"

"Summer better smell good," said Lexie.

"It will," I said. "The best summer-smelling feet ever. Thank you, thank you, thank you!"

"You're welcome," said Lexie.

Chapter seven
Tripped Up

Thursday was a new day. I was dressed up in Lexie's red socks, my white polo shirt, and blue jeans. I was red, white, and blue—just like a flag! I was also going to be honest. And do lots of ten-finger-woo good stuff. Maybe this morning I would get to be flag leader.

Before attendance I went up to Lizzy. She was at her desk. "Do you want to see Gus with me?"

"Yes," she said, looking at the gecko's cage.

"Only I can't." She frowned. "I forgot to do the last row of math problems on our homework."

"Too bad," I said. Because we both love Gus. He's so green and cute in a bug-eyed way.

So I zipped up to Gus by myself. Only my elbows sort of accidentally, maybe, probably, pushed some dictionaries off the table on my way. They thudded with a smack onto the floor. I'd pick them up later. First I had to see my guy Gus.

I opened Gus's cage. He loves it when I pet him and sing a little song about crickets.

"Crickets crunch!" I sang as I stroked his soft belly. "You love crickets a bunch! They're the best lunch! Munch, munch, munch!"

"Ellie May," said Ms. Silva in her not-happy voice. She gave me her Teacher Look and put my clothespin onto orange. My plans to be good went kablooey, even though I was in red, white, and blue!

"But I was singing a happy song," I explained.

"Yes, but you were running. Wash your hands and pick up those books."

Ugh! That's one of our classroom rules. *No Running.*

"Why can't my good thing—singing to Gus—cancel out my bad thing—running and book dropping?" I asked.

Ms. Silva put a hand on my shoulder. "Ellie May, if I catch you doing something else thoughtful, I'll move the clothespin onto green." She smiled at me. And I smiled back. Maybe I really could be flag leader this morning. My teacher doesn't smile when she's super mad and grouchy. This had to be a surefire good sign!

Right after attendance Ms. Silva pointed at the flag in the corner of the classroom. "Who wants to be flag leader?" she asked.

I threw my legs into the center aisle so Ms. Silva could see how Lexie's red socks completed my outfit, and my hand shot right up. So did a whole bunch of other kids' hands. Lizzy's hand stayed down, since she had already gone this month and didn't want to take a turn away from me. I made sure to smile extra big. Lucky for me I had brushed this morning, so my teeth were super shiny and clean. And I looked just like a flag!

Ms. Silva squinted at us like it was sunny inside. "Hmm, lots of hands." She tapped her chin.

Please, please, let it be me.

But I had a warning. My name was on the not-so-good orange square.

But I had also sung a happy cricket song.

Ms. Silva once again smiled right at me. Wow. Could it be my turn? In her clogs she clacked toward my desk. "Mo will be flag leader," she said, putting her hand on Mo's shoulder. I felt extra slumpy. Everyone let out a big ten-finger woo.

While Mo led the pledge, my heart sunk so

low that I thought it might drop to my toes. If I were flag leader I would not whisper the words like Mo. I would say them loud and proud.

That is, if I ever get to be flag leader this week, or again in my lifetime.

When Mo strutted back to his seat, he high-fived Max. Grinning, he sat down next to me and said, "That's the second time this month I've been flag leader!" Then he high-fived himself.

I felt extra fizzled and flat.

Next we had a spelling test. It was hard for me to concentrate on it. I got five answers wrong: *soil*, *weather*, *wear*, *herd*, and *guess*. I spelled them *sewl*, *whether*, *where*, *heard*, and *geuss*. Some of the words were spelled right; they were just the wrong words. Those are the trickiest kind of words. In her smarty-pants voice Ava told me she got everything correct. When she asked me how I did, I wouldn't tell her. But she must've known it wasn't good, because she gave me a pity-party look.

During free read, Ava whizzed over to grab that big fat dictionary so she could show off. She's the only person I know who looks stuff up when she reads. Ms. Silva sometimes gives her a token for it. When you get lots of tokens, you get to pick out something from the treasure box.

But on the way to the bookshelf, Ava tripped. That's when I realized I could be helpful and I could be honest. I could also get back at Ava for being so perfect all the time.

"If I'm going to be honest here, your feet are really big," I told Ava. "That's why you flip-flop all around. You're clumsy. And that's why you fell."

Ava started to sniffle.

"What did I do?" I asked. "I was just being honest."

"My feet aren't too big," said Ava. Her lips puckered, and she darted to her desk.

I skipped over to Max. He needed some honesty too.

"If I can be extremely honest here, you copy and follow Mo all the time." I pointed to the bottle of glue. "I'll glue you two together so you never lose each other."

"Cool!" said Max.

But things weren't cool with Ava. She wasn't at her desk any longer. She was whispering to Ms. Silva by the math center.

Ms. Silva peered over at me. Her forehead wrinkled.

Ava smirked, and she looked really pleased as Ms. Silva strode up to me.

Uh-oh. This was not going to be good.

"You need to apologize to your friend," said Ms. Silva. "You're moving to red."

"Don't I get another warning?" I asked, hoping with all my heart.

She walked over to the behavior chart and clipped my clothespin onto the red square. The bad square. "Ellie May, you owe me five minutes inside during recess."

"Okay," I said, swallowing hard.

"Those were not nice things to say. You can make smarter choices."

I hung my head and whispered, "They always get to be flag leader and I don't. I was just trying to act honest. Like George Washington. I was trying to be like a good president."

"Even presidents aren't perfect," Ms. Silva said. "Maybe you could try to be your own kind of honest. The kind of honest that doesn't hurt people's feelings." I felt all slumpy again.

Chapter Eight
Read All About It

Even though Ms. Silva said all presidents weren't perfect, at least they weren't boring. Not boring at all. During the rest of free read, I read books about all the presidents. I learned lots of stuff.

Ava scooted around in her chair and seemed to be studying *me*.

"I'm not doing anything wrong," I protested, holding up a book. "I'm reading. *See?*"

"I just wanted to know what you were reading." She shrugged. "You kept on saying, 'Wow.'"

"Oh." Usually Ava turned around to shush me. "Well, I'm learning cool stuff about presidents. President Obama loves comics and was born on an island with volcanoes. It's called—"

"Hawaii," filled in Ava.

"That's right! And President Reagan loved jellybeans. His favorite flavor was licorice."

Ava made a face. "Yuck."

"I know," I said. "President Carter was a peanut farmer. That means he's nutty."

Ava smiled. "That's silly." Ava cracked up. She may be a Miss Know-It-All, but she likes my jokes. "Ellie May, you're really into this."

"I know." I scooped up one of the books off my desk. "You should read this. I've already finished it."

"Thanks," she said.

"You're welcome," I said.

Right away Ava opened up the book I'd given her, which didn't make me feel slumpy at all.

I went back to learning not-boring facts about the two biggies: George Washington and Abraham Lincoln. I wrote down my favorite facts.

Cool Facts About George Washington

1) He didn't wear a wig. It was real hair but powdered white. He fluffed and curled it and put it in a ponytail so he'd look cool.
(Cool used to look different way back then.)

2) He had no middle name.

3) He loved writing letters and wrote almost 20,000 of them. In some of the letters, he talked about how honesty was a big deal.

4) He wasn't liked by everyone. Thomas Jefferson wasn't a big fan, and some people today aren't either. (I guess Ms. Silva was right about every president not being perfect.)

5) He loved dogs. Two of his dogs were named True Love and Sweet Lips.

6) He had false teeth, made from gold, lead, hippo teeth, cow teeth, and donkey teeth! Or at least some historians think he did.

Woohoo! I was like George Washington because I had false vampire teeth for Halloween, we both love dogs, and we both have lots of curls in our hair. I was not like him because I have a middle name, and I'm not so sure if I like writing letters.

But maybe I could write a letter just like him. I looked up at the clock above the white board; it was snack time. Snack time was only fifteen minutes long. That didn't give me much time.

I raced over to my cubby and yanked my fruit chew out of my lunchbox. I gobbled it extra quick.

Next to me Lizzy pulled an applesauce out of her backpack. "Want to draw fairies?"

"No, thanks. I'm going to write a letter. Just like George Washington!"

"Can't you do that later?" she asked.

"I have to finish it today. But I can draw during recess. And after school we can play fairies at my

house," I said. "And Midge can be our magic cat."
Midge loved to pretend to be a cat.

"Okay," said Lizzy. "I'll draw a cat right now
and give it magical powers."

"Cool!" I said. But I couldn't think of anything
to write. I wished I had magical writing powers.

"Do you have any more Fruit Roll-ups?"
asked Pablo. We're desk partners.

I pointed to my tummy. "All gone."

"Too bad," he said. "I was going to trade you
this." He shook his bag of barbecue potato chips.
They smelled so good and salty. I tried to get back
to writing, only my pencil tip broke.

I dashed over to the pencil sharpener and stood
behind Jamila. She neighed. I neighed back. When
my pencil was good and pointy, I scrambled back
to my desk and stared at the blank page.

Wait. What if I wrote a letter to Ms. Silva
from George Washington? What if I told her who

would be a good flag leader? She'd listen to him. Because he was the first president!

I slipped the letter in the mailbox. It's not a real mailbox. It's a classroom box where you can put your letters to Ms. Silva.

I couldn't wait until she read George's letter!

Deer Ms. Silva,

I am writing to you today. It is very importent. Everything I say is very importent. That is because I am the president. Well, I was the president. I am not the president now. That is because I am not alive.

Don't worry. I am not a ghost. I am just writing a letter. I love letters.

My name is George. Your students study me.

I want to tell you about a girl.

She has curly hair. And wears flag colors. Maybe even red socks. She risked a lot for those socks. That is because she wanted to look like a flag. I think she looks more like a flag than any other child in this class.

You couldn't ask for a kid who looks more like a flag in the whole entyre country.

She even had her little sister be a flag.

This is the kind of person who would make a great flag leader for this great classroom.

Sincerly,

George Washington

(Who is not alive but if I were, this is what I would write.)

P.S. Even though I didn't chop down a cherry tree, I like cherries.

Chapter Nine
Rainy-Day Recess

It started to rain, so we had to take our recess inside. It's called rainy-day recess. That means we sit inside our classroom while rain drips, drips, drips outside. We don't get them too much, so it's special.

I zoomed over to Lizzy by the art table. Only Ms. Silva put her hand on my shoulder. "Ellie May, it's time now for you to go sit at your desk. Please sit still and don't talk to anyone for five minutes."

"Okay," I said. My shoulders went slumpy. I had forgotten all about my punishment for telling Ava about her big feet.

Sitting still was really boring. Kids played board games and snuggled on beanbag chairs in the reader corner. My legs wanted to go wiggly so bad.

But then something not so boring happened.

Ms. Silva walked over to the mailbox. *Creak!* The mailbox door opened. She grabbed the George Washington letter. *Wowie!*

Now I really needed to turn my head to look at her. Jamila and the horse girls galloped past my desk. Craning my neck, I watched Ms. Silva.

She held the letter in her hand.

She was reading it, really and truly.

Her lips didn't go into a smile. But they also didn't get frowny. What did that mean? What did she think of the letter?

Ms. Silva peered at me. My heart went skittery fast. "Ellie May . . . ," she began.

"Yes?" I popped up out of my seat. Was she going to announce me as flag leader a whole day early?

"Your time is up," finished Ms. Silva. "You may get out of your seat. Well, I see that you have already. But you may now join the rest of the class for indoor recess."

Lizzy smiled and motioned for me to join her.

Only I didn't feel super smiley at all.

"Thanks," I said to Ms. Silva before plodding over to the art table. I plopped across from Lizzy and began scribbling a really crazy-looking fairy. I grabbed a blue marker out of the art bucket to make some blue hair. To make it crazier.

"What's wrong?" asked Lizzy.

"Nothing," I said, looking back at Ms. Silva.

"Something's up," insisted Lizzy.

"It's just that your fairy is super-duper good, Lizzy."

"Thanks," she said as Owen whizzed past, a paper airplane in his hand.

It was true. Her fairy looked realistic. Not that fairies are real. But if they were, they would look like Lizzy's fairies. With sparkly dresses, wands with stars, and bubble-gum-pink wings.

"My fairy looks like a blue bug," I grumbled.

"That's okay," said Lizzy, studying my drawing. "It can be the fairy's pet."

"A blue bumblebee," I said, "and it can sting the bad guys."

"Yes, and make honey for the fairies." Lizzy grabbed a yellow pen. "I'll draw a hive."

"Thanks," I said, turning around to look at Ms. Silva. She hadn't let on about whether she knew it was me who wrote that letter. For all Ms. Silva knew, another kid could have written it.

"Why do you keep looking over there?" Lizzy asked.

I sighed the biggest sigh. "Just waiting for my big break," I told Lizzy.

I watched Ms. Silva give blue and green pens to Jamila for the white board. During rainy-day recess, Ms. Silva lets us draw on the boards.

Right now I wanted to draw a big message on that white board. I'd write: *What should I do next?*

Chapter Ten
Gadget
Gone Wrong

There was no way to know if my letter from George Washington was going to get me picked for flag leader. And I couldn't just stare at Ms. Silva all day, waiting for her to give me a sign. So I got back to research. Turns out there were lots of amazing facts about Abraham Lincoln too. I started a new list.

Cool Facts About Abraham Lincoln

1) He was a wrestler.

2) He loved cats.

3) He was the first president with a beard.

4) Some people say he used his power too much when he was president. (Ms. Silva would probably want me to look into this more, using lots of different books.)

5) He had no middle name.

6) He liked gadgets and taking them apart to see how they worked.

My latest list made me realize something huge. I had to get rid of my middle name. Both George Washington and Abraham Lincoln did not have a middle name. May is a silly name anyway. It's the name of a regular month. And not a really good month, like December, when getting major gifts happens, or February, when Presidents' Day happens.

The best fact of all? I was also like Abraham Lincoln because I like gadgets.

And taking them apart, just like he did. I looked around the classroom. What could I take apart?

During science free choice, kids swarmed the nature center. But there was nothing to take apart except nature stuff. Other kids were doing art. Still others were working on the word wall.

Ms. Silva has a coffeemaker behind her desk. Plus a camera and an iPad. She'd never let me touch those.

Then I heard it. *Whirr, whirr, shhh. Whirr, whirr, shhh.* Our classroom pencil sharpener!

It sat next to the math center. Ms. Silva was busy circling the class to talk about all the science-y stuff we could look at. So I decided to peer inside that pencil sharpener. It was nice and full.

I twisted it this way. I twisted it that way.

I got the whole thing apart and felt super-duper proud.

Ava hustled over to me. "What are you doing, Ellie May?" she whispered.

"My name isn't Ellie May anymore. It's just Ellie. And I'm being like Lincoln!" I said in a very loud voice so Ms. Silva could hear.

Lizzy gave me a strange look, since everyone always *always* calls me Ellie May.

But Ms. Silva wasn't listening. She was talking to Pablo.

I put down all the parts of the sharpener and scooted back to my seat. When Ms. Silva was done talking to Pablo, she gazed over at the floor next to the math center. "Who did this?" She stared at the pencil sharpener parts. She glared at the mess all over the rug. Pencil shavings were littered everywhere. *Uh-oh!* That was a big kablooey!

If I told Ms. Silva it was me, she could put my clothespin onto the purple square. That means a call home. Then I wouldn't become flag leader tomorrow. I would be the bad-square leader.

I waited. Who had seen me? Ava had.

"Who did this?" asked Ms. Silva. "Please come forward."

Ava looked at me.

She didn't say anything. I was in shock. This might have been the first time in her life she hadn't told on someone. I wondered if she was being so nice because I had shared all those cool books with her.

I didn't say anything either.

Ms. Silva sighed. She clacked to her desk and cut little slips of paper. Handing them out, she said, "Please write down either *yes* or *no*. Yes, you did take apart the sharpener and leave shavings on the floor, or, no, you didn't. Then write your name." I studied my blank slip of paper.

What would a good president do?

Chapter Eleven
Never Ever

On my slip of paper, I slowly wrote:

I messed up the pencil sharpener because it's a gadgit. Lincoln liked gadgits and taking them apart. And I want to be like him. But I also want to tell the truth now, because I want to act like a good president. I am so so SO sorry.

Ellie ~~May~~

Now I would never ever get to be flag leader before Presidents' Day. Tomorrow, Friday, was my last chance, and it felt hopeless!

Right now the only kind of leader I would be was a bad-behavior leader.

Ms. Silva stood behind her desk and looked right at me. She pointed to the floor. "If you took it apart, put it back together."

I swallowed extra hard. It felt like there was a cherry pit stuck in my throat. While everyone else gobbled up their afternoon snack, I looked at each little part of the sharpener. Gradually, I fit the pieces back together like a puzzle. Then I swept up all the pencil shavings. Ms. Silva watched me and gave me a thumbs-up. She didn't put my clothespin on the purple square. But I bet she would soon enough.

I decided to write Ava a letter during the end of snack break. This time I would write it as

myself. Not as George Washington. Not as Lincoln. Not even as the future flag leader of the class. Ava would have to hear from just me, plain old Ellie May.

Dear Ava,

Thank you so much for not telling on me about the pencil sharpener. You could have told Ms. Silva. You could have told other kids. You could have gotten me in big trouble. But you didn't. You were not a tattle tail.

Thank you. You won't have to be a tattle tail any more. I pledge to tell the truth!

And that is not a mith!

Sincerely,
Ellie ~~May~~

Chapter Twelve
They're Alive

At the end of Thursday, after our station activity, it was time to show our posters of symbols. But I didn't feel like sharing.

Mo and Max held up their posters of money. Max pointed to the dollar bill. "This is George Washington."

Then Mo pointed to more money. "This is Abraham Lincoln. He's now a penny and a five-dollar bill. Great presidents become money. Someday I want to become money too."

"Me too," said Max.

A bunch of their friends cheered.

Ava went next. She pointed to her poster. "This is a bald eagle. It is on the seal of the president of the United States. It's at the top of every letter they write. It is considered a symbol for the president. You might want to know why it's called a bald eagle when it's so obviously not bald. It's because *bald* comes from a really old word—*piebald*. For your information, this means having white patches."

"Wow, good research, Ava," said Ms. Silva. Everyone clapped. My teacher loves research. Ava would definitely be flag leader tomorrow.

"Ellie," said Ms. Silva. "it's your turn."

"You can call me Ellie May now," I said.

"It doesn't matter." I didn't think there was any

chance I would be flag leader tomorrow anyway, so there was no longer a need to sound like a president.

I didn't want to get up in front of the class ever again. I didn't want to show anyone my poster. But I had to. "It's a picture of the flag," I said, "kind of like the first one that was around all the way back when George Washington was president. The flag today has thirteen stripes and fifty stars. It used to have fewer stripes and more stars, because there used to be not so many states. And, a real long time ago, the founders of the country tried out other flags. One had a rattlesnake on it with big fangs. Lucky for us, we have the stars-and-stripes kind. Not one with poison on it."

A few kids laughed.

But not me. I sat down and felt fizzled and flat. I wasn't looking forward to tomorrow. Who would be flag leader? I knew that answer.

Not me.

After the bell, Lizzy and I walked down the hallway together to the bus. We were smushed in between a bazillion kids. Principal Lopez stood in front of the door with her orange vest and whistle.

"No running in the halls," she said.

I didn't want to run anywhere right then.

I felt way super slumpy. "Tomorrow's my last shot to be flag leader," I said.

"That's not true, Ellie May," said Lizzy. "You have the rest of the year to be flag leader."

A group of first-grade boys bumped me with their superhero backpacks.

"Slow down," called out Principal Lopez.

"Lizzy, you don't understand," I said. "This will be the last time in my life on planet Earth that I will be a second grader, in this class, during our special Presidents' Day week. Never again!"

I stopped in front of the water fountain and took

a drink. "And what have we been doing? Studying presidents? We have been studying freedom, truth, and symbols." I wiped my mouth with the back of my hand. "I want to be a leader. Not just a regular one either. A flag leader *this* week. But there's no way it can happen."

Then I started to march like I was in a parade. "I just wanted to go up to the front of the class tomorrow. Not pretending to be a president, but as a real person!"

"But you *are* a real person," said Lizzy.

"I know." I put my hand on my chest. I could feel my own heart. It went *ga-thump, ga-thump.* "I think that's the reason you put your hand over your heart when you say the pledge. So you can remember it's all real. Your heart and the flag. They're alive!"

We stepped outside to the drive-in circle where the buses waited. The sky looked puffy and

78

white. Like it wanted to cry rain. "Wow, Ellie May," said Lizzy. "I'd vote for you for flag leader. I see how much it means to you. What you just said sounded really good."

"It did?" I looked for my bus.

"Yes," said Lizzy, "it did. Because it sounded just like you. Ellie May. My best friend in the whole world."

Getting picked for flag leader still felt hopeless, but at least I had Lizzy on my side.

chapter Thirteen
Friday Morning

"Want me to tickle you, Ellie May?" said Lizzy on Friday morning.

"Why?" I asked.

"So you'll smile," she said.

"Nothing can get me to smile." I hung up my backpack. And plopped in my desk.

I didn't even visit Gus the Gecko. I didn't scream out "Present!" when Ms. Silva took attendance. I didn't wear my red socks. Instead I wore a gray shirt and purple leggings. I didn't look like an American flag at all.

"Who wants to be flag leader on this final day during our week of studying presidents?" Ms. Silva asked.

Ava raised her hand.

Mo raised his hand. And Max. And Jamila and, well, everybody except for Lizzy, who was trying to be nice.

I didn't raise my hand either. There was no use.

I closed my eyes. I plugged my ears. I couldn't listen.

Suddenly I felt a hand on my shoulder. I opened my eyes.

"Ellie May," said Ms. Silva, smiling a really big smile. "You're our flag leader this last day before Presidents' Day."

Everyone stared at me.

Ava gave me a thumbs-up.

My mouth dropped open. "But I was the one who took apart the sharpener."

"Yes." Ms. Silva tapped the tip of her very sharp pencil. "But you admitted to it and put it back together. And you also wrote a very nice letter in the style of George Washington. It sounded quite presidential. That's why you're our flag leader today."

Everyone gave me a big ten-finger woo. Lizzy cheered the loudest.

I felt dizzy with happiness. Like I'd just been elected president of the class—or the entire United States. If I were a flag, I'd be flapping extra hard. This was the biggest and best surprise ever!

I clapped my hands and whooped before strolling to the front of the class. I stood tall and lifted my chin.

Everyone was quiet.

They all looked at me, Ellie May, flag leader
right before Presidents' Day.

I raised my hand over my heart and began.

I pledge allegiance
to the flag
of the United States of America
and to the Republic for which it stands,
one Nation
under God,
indivisible,
with liberty and justice for all.

chapter fourteen
an on-the-money presidents' Day

Presidents' Day weekend was crazy busy, as usual. We had to go to Lexie's boring swim meet where a bunch of kids swam laps for hours and hours. Then we had to run to the grocery store to buy yogurt and prune juice, the yuckiest kind of juice in the world.

But Monday was free! And the best thing about having no school on Presidents' Day was

that my whole entire family was home. Mom
didn't have to go to work at her office. Dad didn't
have to write a story on deadline. Midge didn't
need to go to daycare. Lexie didn't have to be at
swim practice. And I didn't have to worry about
being a flag leader anymore.

Lexie, Midge, and I decided to get our money
together. We wanted to buy cupcake batter at the
store. When I counted my money in my piggy
bank, I looked at a penny in a whole new way.
A penny has Lincoln's head on it. A nickel has
Jefferson's. George Washington is on the quarter.
I always knew they were on money, but now I
knew that they were real and had done things for
our country. I still had so much to learn about
each of them.

While Midge played a card game with Mom,
Lexie and I walked together to the corner store.
Well, I skipped and Lexie walked.

"Seventh graders don't skip," she said.

"Then seventh graders are boring," I said, skipping even faster.

"We need icing and cupcakes," I said to the man behind the counter when we reached the store. "But not the already-made kind. The stuff in a box."

"In the second aisle," said the cashier.

"It's called cake mix," hissed Lexie. She grabbed a cake mix box and a container of icing.

Lexie put her dollar bills down on the counter, and I handed over my one hundred pennies and seven nickels.

"Here you go," I said.

The guy behind the counter smiled. "You're right on the money."

"No, I'm not," I said. "George Washington, Thomas Jefferson, and Abraham Lincoln are on the money."

"Please ignore my sister," begged Lexie.

"Have a cozy, on-the-money Presidents' Day," I said as we walked out of the store

On the way home the sky was cloudy. It looked like toothpaste. I liked that because it looked clean and fresh.

In the backyard Dad was hanging up the flag. And Diesel was trying to help him.

Mom was grilling chicken and zucchini. It was a warm day even for winter in California.

Lexie, Midge, and I got out bowls and spoons and made the cake mix. We were already dressed in red, white, and blue. I had Lexie's red socks on again, because she said I hadn't even stunk them up last time I wore them. Whew!

As I was icing the cupcakes, I had to get the answer to one important question. "What do you call someone who isn't president any more?" I asked.

"President," said Lexie.

"Well, you can call them ex-president," said Mom, wiping barbecue sauce from her hands. They smelled sweet and spicy.

"Or you could call them former presidents," said Dad, shaking out a tablecloth.

"Hey, that means I am an ex-flag leader," I announced. "Or a former flag leader before Presidents' Weekend. That is the best kind of flag leader, because it means I've already done it."

"And you're free," said Mom, "since you've done your duty."

I spread my arms out in a victory salute. "Yes! And I learned a lot of presidential facts."

"That sounds boring," said Midge. She plopped down on the ground to pet Diesel.

"Now you can take a flag-leader vacation, Ellie May," Mom said.

"Or she could write her memoir," said Dad.

"What's a mem-*wah*?" asked Midge.

"It's a story," said Dad. "A story about your life."

"You could write mine for me," I said to Dad. "Since you're a writer."

"Well, no." Dad shook his head. "A memoir is different from a biography. A memoir you write about yourself."

"That sounds boring, boring, boring," sang Midge in a singsongy voice.

"Mine wouldn't be boring," I said. "Because in my memoir there would be plants getting chopped, pencil sharpeners that get taken apart, and flag leading." I turned to my dad. "How do you start a memoir exactly?" I asked.

"Well, you start by writing down stories of your life. Whatever comes to you first," said Dad.

"I have lots of stories," I said. "I could write a whole book of stuff."

Lexie rolled her eyes.

"I bet you could," said Mom.

"I could write all the ways I worked hard to make sure I would be flag leader last week, even when I never thought I'd get picked," I said.

"I want to write a book about cupcakes!" screamed Midge.

"That's a delicious idea," said Mom.

"And I could write about how crazy my family is," said Lexie.

"You won't think so when I'm giving autographs," I said. "I could sell my memoir at the White House on Presidents' Day." I hopped up onto a chair and thrust a wooden spoon into the air. "I officially declare it's been a great Presidents' Day. I pledge cupcakes for everyone!" Diesel wagged his tail. "And for puppies too!"

"Okay, Madame President," Mom said. "It's time to test the cupcakes."

"Yes," I said, hopping down and rubbing my belly. "I'll be the leader here and taste-test them first."

The Pledge of Allegiance

The Pledge of Allegiance is part of the fabric of our country. The Pledge was first published in a children's magazine. The owner of the magazine was concerned that after the Civil War, the United States was divided. He wanted the Pledge to unify the country, and he hoped to see American flags in every public school.

While the Pledge has gone through many changes, the goal is to affirm the values of the United States. Some of these core values include liberty and justice.

Presidents' Day

The freely elected leader of the United States
is the president. Presidents' Day began as a party
to celebrate the birthday of George Washington
in 1796. Soon the holiday became popular. Each
year, on February 22, the country celebrated
with parties across the land and dances called
Birthnight Balls.

After President Abraham Lincoln's
assassination in 1865, the nation commemorated
his birthday on February 12. Many states made
Lincoln's birthday a holiday. In 1968 Congress
changed the celebration of Washington's birthday
to the third Monday in February, and this has
become known as Presidents' Day. This holiday
honors Lincoln and Washington, as well as all the
presidents who have served the United States.

Every year classrooms across the country make February the official month to learn more about the highest office in America and all about presidents. Some classrooms celebrate by putting up posters, completing crafts, learning about the flag, discussing how the government works, and reading books.

What does your school do to celebrate this special day?

99

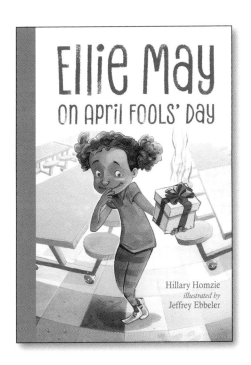

ELLie May
ON APRiL FOOLS' DAY

Hillary Homzie
illustrated by
Jeffrey Ebbeler